Fairy stories hold a fascination for children that cannot be equalled. This story has been adapted for beginner readers but if your child is not able to read, you can read this delightful story aloud. For your child, listening to a story in a relaxed atmosphere is a vital part of the learning process. For you, the reader, there is the opportunity to discuss the feelings the story conjures up and the meanings of any unfamiliar words with your child.

Linda Coates Cert Ed, MA.

Snow White and the Seven Dwarfs

retold by Brenda Apsley
illustrated by Gill Guile

Published in Great Britain by World International Publishing Limited,
An Egmont Company, Egmont House, P.O. Box 111, Great Ducie Street, Manchester M60 3BL
Printed in Italy. SBN 7235 8763 9

Once, in a land far away, there lived a king and queen. They had one daughter, a lovely child with soft white skin and hair as black as coal. She was called Snow White.

Snow White's mother died when she was young, and soon the king married again. But his new wife was cruel and unkind. She was very jealous of Snow White's beauty.

The queen had a magic mirror. When she asked, "Mirror, mirror, on the wall, who is the fairest of them all?" the mirror always replied that the queen was the fairest of all.

As the years passed Snow White grew from a lovely child into a beautiful young woman. She was good and kind and everyone loved her — everyone except the queen.

One day the queen asked her magic mirror, "Mirror, mirror on the wall, who is the fairest of them all?" But this time the mirror said that Snow White was the fairest!

The queen flew into a terrible rage and called her servant. "Take Snow White far into the forest and kill her!" she ordered. "I never want to see her again!"

The servant took Snow White into the forest, but he could not kill her for he knew that she had done nothing wrong. He told her to run far away so the queen would not find her.

Snow White wandered through the dark forest for many hours until at last she came to a tiny cottage. She decided to ask the people who lived there to help her.

She knocked on the door. When there was no reply, she went inside, where she found a small table and seven tiny chairs. On the table were seven tiny mugs and seven tiny plates.

Snow White climbed the stairs to the bedroom, and there she found seven small beds. She was so tired that she lay across the beds to rest and very soon fell fast asleep.

Snow White was still sleeping when the seven dwarfs who lived in the cottage returned that night. They wondered who she was, and what she was doing in their cottage.

When Snow White woke up she stared in surprise at the seven little men. They looked good and kind so she told them her story and the dwarfs asked her to stay with them.

Snow White was happy living with the seven dwarfs. She cooked for them, mended and washed their clothes, and kept the house clean. The seven dwarfs grew to love her.

Early each morning they went off to work in their gold mine. “Don’t speak to anyone,” they warned her. “You will be safe as long as the queen thinks you are dead.”

But when the wicked queen asked her magic mirror, "Mirror, mirror, on the wall, who is the fairest of them all?" the mirror replied that Snow White was still the fairest.

So the queen disguised herself as an old woman and collected a basket of apples from the kitchen. She filled one of the apples with poison.

The evil queen followed the path that led into the forest and after a few hours found the dwarfs' cottage. "She must be living here," said the queen.

The queen knocked at the door of the cottage. Snow White would not open it, but the old woman begged her. "Please try one of my apples. I have walked for many hours to bring them to you."

Snow White felt sorry for the old woman, and at last she opened the door, took the shiny red apple from the old woman's hand and put it to her lips. But as she bit the poisoned apple, she fell to the floor.

When the seven dwarfs returned from the gold mine that night they found Snow White lying where she had fallen. They knew she wasn't dead, but they could not wake her.

The dwarfs put Snow White in a glass coffin and carried it into the forest. They laid the coffin in a shady glade among the trees and guarded it day and night.

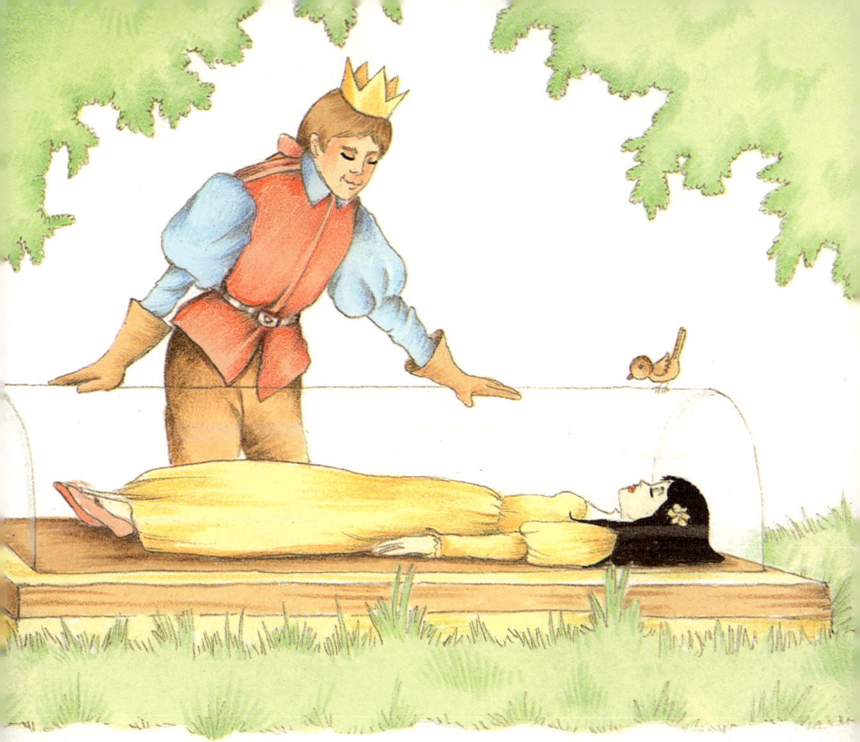

Some months later, a prince saw the glass coffin and asked the dwarfs if he could look at the beautiful girl inside it. As he looked at Snow White's pale face, the prince fell in love with her.

He bent over to kiss Snow White, and as his lips touched hers the piece of poisoned apple fell from her mouth! Snow White woke up, and when she saw the handsome prince she fell in love with him.

Soon, Snow White and the prince were married in the prince's palace on the far side of the forest. There were seven very special guests at the wedding — the seven dwarfs.